2 Corinthians 5:7
"For we walk by faith, not by sight."

Dedicated to Alex and the entire Makimei Children's Home located in Nairobi, Kenya. Thank you for showing me how effortlessly it is to smile; even through the challenging times.

FAITH OVER SIGHT

By Serena Haeuser

What if you could not use your eyes?

Unable to see the sky, or even the pretty birds that fly by.

You cannot see your friends clearly, or the yummy vegetables your mother puts on your plate that you love so dearly.

But better yet; imagine always being happy, rather than walking around looking all sappy.

But, how so? Your toy is not big enough. Your sneakers have too many scruffs. You simply believe that you do not have enough stuff.

Tough right? I wonder how Alex does it.

He never comes out to play. He stays in the house with his mama all day. The neighborhood kids never understood. Alex not playing outside at times he should.

No tag, no basketball, nor participating in any race.
But whenever they see him, he sure does have a big
smile on his face.

When Lucy passes by, she can see Alex and his mother sitting at the dinner table together; hand in hand.

And at times, when Benjamin flies by he can see Mama Margaret; Alex's mother, with her hands held high to the sky.

One day, Lucy decided to knock at Alex's door. She was greeted by Mama Margaret.

Good evening Mama Margaret. I wanted to ask, why doesn't Alex ever come outside? To at least play with us on the slide.

"Lucy, sweetie," Mama Margaret began. Lucy interrupted; "he is the happiest person that I know. Whenever I see him it is like he has this big glow."

Mama Margaret chuckled.
"I taught Alex something when he was very young. Here in our household, we call that faith," she explained. Lucy looked puzzled. "What does that mean?"

"Well Lucy, nothing is ever as bad as it may seem. Although my son cannot walk nor see, we are very blessed and have God on our team. Alex is alive! We strongly believe that he will be able to do those things one day and strive."

"Plus, that is what faith is all about! Never having any doubts."

Count   Your

Blessings

A Letter to Alex:

Dear Alex,

I pray that we get to meet again one day and I can share this story with you.
I pray that you never lose that sparkle of yours and you never stop being you.
I pray that your sight comes back, and can see for yourself how contagious that smile of yours is.
I pray that you never give up no matter what; you are one of the chosen ones.
Alex; I thank you for everything that you and your beautiful country instilled in me during my time there.
I will never forget it.
I will never forget you.
Faith Over Sight.
-Serena Haeuser

Made in the USA
Middletown, DE
10 June 2020